Pink Princess
COOKBOOK

Barbara Beery

Gibbs Smith, Publisher
Salt Lake City

First Edition
10 09 08 07 06   5 4 3 2 1

Text © 2006 Barbara Beery
Photographs © 2006 Marty Snortum

Cover design by Dawn DeVries Sokol
Interior design by Sheryl Dickert Smith
Food styling by Katie Beck

Published by
Gibbs Smith, Publisher
P.O. Box 667
Layton, Utah 84041

Orders: 1.800.748.5439
www.gibbs-smith.com

Printed and bound in Hong Kong

Library of Congress Control Number: 2006926510

ISBN 1-4236-0173-4

Contents

Angel Cloud Cakes

Ingredients List

1 package angel food cake mix

1 teaspoon vanilla

½ teaspoon almond extract

¼ cup confetti sprinkles

2 to 3 cups whipped cream or whipped topping

1 cup flaked coconut

Makes 24 cupcakes

Let's get baking!

Preheat oven to 350 degrees.

Make cake mix according to package directions, adding vanilla and almond extract.

Mix on low speed for about 1 minute, then mix on medium for 1 more minute.

Fold in confetti sprinkles.

Line two 12-cup cupcake pans with foil cupcake liners. Spoon batter into each cup, filling three-fourths full. Bake about 25 minutes or until the tops are dark golden brown. Do not underbake.

Carefully remove cupcakes from oven and cool in pan 5 minutes. Remove from cupcake pans and cool at least 1 hour before frosting.

Frost with "clouds" of whipped cream on each cupcake and sprinkle with coconut.

These taste heavenly!

Pink Princess Cake

Ingredients List

For cake:

½ cup butter, softened

1 cup sugar

2 eggs

2 teaspoons vanilla

Pink gel food coloring

½ cup milk

¼ teaspoon salt

2 teaspoons baking powder

1½ cups all-purpose flour

For frosting:

¼ cup butter, softened

4 cups powdered sugar

2 tablespoons milk (more if frosting is too stiff)

1 teaspoon vanilla

Pink gel food coloring

Confetti sprinkles

Makes 1 round
2-layer cake

Let's get baking!

Preheat oven to 350 degrees.

In a medium-sized bowl, cream together butter and sugar with an electric mixer. Beat in eggs, one at a time. Then stir in vanilla.

Stir a small amount of pink food coloring into the milk and set aside. In another bowl, combine salt, baking powder, and flour. Add to batter alternately with colored milk. Beat until smooth and creamy, about 1 minute.

Divide batter between one 8-inch round cake pan and one 6-inch round cake pan, each sprayed generously with nonstick cooking spray and lined with circles of waxed paper or parchment paper.

Bake 30 to 35 minutes. The smaller cake may be done a few minutes before the bigger cake. Cakes should be golden brown. When touched lightly, they should not leave fingerprints.

Cool in pans 10 to 15 minutes, then carefully remove by placing a plate or rack over each cake pan and inverting the cake onto it. Cool another 10 to 15 minutes before frosting.

When cakes are cool, center smaller cake on top of larger one.

To make the frosting, beat butter in a large bowl with an electric mixer. Slowly add powdered sugar, one-half cup at a time, alternately with milk. Add vanilla.

Stir in a tiny bit of pink gel food coloring. Add extra milk, 1 tablespoon at a time, if necessary.

Frost and decorate with sprinkles.

A cake fit for a princess!

Sweet Berry Shortcakes

Ingredients List

For shortcakes:

1 package frozen puff
   pastry dough

2 tablespoons butter,
   melted

2 tablespoons sugar

For berries:

1½ to 2 cups raspberries,
   blueberries, and sliced
   strawberries

1 tablespoon sugar

½ teaspoon vanilla

For topping:

Whipped cream

Assorted berries for
   garnish

Makes 4 to 5
servings

Let's get baking!

Thaw dough for 30 minutes before using.

Preheat oven to 375 degrees.

Open one sheet of puff pastry and place on floured work area. Gently roll out and smooth pastry.

Use a cookie cutter to cut out a total of 12 to 15 pastries.

Place individual pastries on a foil-lined cookie sheet sprayed with nonstick cooking spray. Brush pastries lightly with melted butter, and sprinkle lightly with sugar.

Bake for about 15 minutes. Remove from oven and cool for 5 minutes before removing from cookie sheet.

Combine assorted berries, sugar, and vanilla in a bowl. Set aside.

Place one puff pastry round on a plate and spoon berries on top.

Put a second pastry round on top of that and add more berries.

Top with a third pastry round. Finish off with a dollop of whipped cream and assorted berries.

If your shortcake stack begins to slide, secure each pastry round to the next with a toothpick. Be careful not to bite the toothpicks!

This dessert is "berry" delicious!

Cotton Candy Cupcakes

Ingredients List

1 package strawberry or white cake mix

Milk

½ teaspoon vanilla

Pink gel food coloring

1 16-ounce container prepared vanilla frosting

2 bags purchased cotton candy

Makes 24 cupcakes

Let's get baking!

Preheat oven to 350 degrees.

Make cake mix according to package directions, substituting milk for water and adding vanilla.

Line two cupcake pans with pink paper cupcake liners. Divide batter evenly between liners. Bake according to package directions.

Cool cupcakes 10 to 15 minutes.

Meanwhile, in a medium bowl stir 1 to 2 drops of pink gel food coloring into prepared frosting. Blend well. Then frost cupcakes.

Divide cotton candy into 24 small sections and set each one on top of a frosted cupcake.

Float away on a cotton candy cloud!

Ginger Cookies

Ingredients List

For cookies:

¾ cup butter, softened

½ cup packed brown sugar

1 egg

¾ cup molasses

½ teaspoon cloves

2 teaspoons ginger

½ teaspoon nutmeg

1 teaspoon cinnamon

¼ teaspoon salt

3 cups all-purpose flour

Powdered sugar for rolling
   out dough

Makes 24 cookies

Let's get baking!

Preheat oven to 350 degrees.

In a large bowl, combine butter, brown sugar, egg, and molasses.

Stir in dry ingredients except powdered sugar and mix completely. Cover bowl and refrigerate for 2 to 3 hours.

Remove cookie dough from refrigerator and take small portions of the dough, about ¼ cup to ½ cup, and roll out to ¼ to ½ inch thick. Use powdered sugar instead of flour to roll out cookie dough. It won't toughen cookies as flour does if too much is used.

Cut out with assorted cookie cutters and place on a foil-lined cookie sheet sprayed with non-stick cooking spray. Bake for 8 to 12 minutes, depending on size of cookie.

To make Decorator Frosting, combine meringue powder, powdered sugar, water, vanilla, and almond extract in a mixing bowl.

For decorator frosting:

3 tablespoons commercial
  meringue powder

2 cups powdered sugar

¼ cup plus 2 tablespoons
  warm water

1 teaspoon vanilla

½ teaspoon almond extract

Food coloring

For decorating:

Assorted candies and
  decorating sprinkles

Beat on high speed with an electric mixer for
3 to 5 minutes.

Divide in separate bowls and add drops of food
color as desired.

Let cookies cool on cookie sheet for 5 minutes,
then carefully remove. Cool another 10 minutes
before frosting and decorating.

Fortune Cookies

Good fortune is coming your way!

Ingredients List

2 to 3 tablespoons cornstarch sprinkled on work area

1 package refrigerated piecrusts

1 tablespoon water

Colored decorating sugars, placed in small saucers

Makes 12 fortune cookies

Let's get baking!

Preheat oven to 350 degrees.

Write a note of good fortune or draw little symbols (a sun, moon, heart, or flower) on two-inch-long pieces of paper with a pen or non-toxic marker.

Sprinkle cornstarch on your work area and smooth it with your hand.

Unfold one piecrust at a time and place on work area. Turn over crust to dust both sides with cornstarch. Flatten and smooth out wrinkles with rolling pin. With a 3-inch-round cookie cutter, cut out 4 to 6 circles per piecrust. You may reroll scraps if you wish.

Put one fortune in the center of each circle and fold in half. Then fold the semicircle in half.

Brush each fortune cookie with a little water to moisten. Dip one side of each cookie into a colored sugar, then place on cookie sheet, sugar-side-up. Place cookies 2 inches apart.

Bake for 15 to 20 minutes or until lightly browned. Carefully take from oven and cool 5 minutes before removing from pan.

Totally-Tea-Cake Cookies

Ingredients List

For cookies:

½ cup butter or margarine, softened

¾ cup sugar

1 egg

¾ teaspoon vanilla

2 cups all-purpose flour

½ teaspoon baking soda

½ teaspoon salt

For frosting:

One recipe Decorator Frosting (see page 15)

Decorating sugars

Makes 36 cookies

Let's get baking!

Preheat oven to 375 degrees.

Cream butter or margarine in a large mixing bowl. Add sugar, beating until light and fluffy. Add egg and vanilla, mixing well.

Combine flour, baking soda, and salt in a separate bowl. Add to creamed mixture, blending well. Dough will be very stiff.

Divide dough into thirds. Roll each portion to ⅛ inch thick on lightly floured work area. Cut with assorted cookie cutters. Place cookies 2 inches apart on cookie sheets sprayed with nonstick cooking spray.

Bake for 8 to 10 minutes or until lightly browned. Remove to wire racks to cool. Frost and decorate as desired.

Make these for your next tea party!

Pink Princess Crown Cookies

Ingredients List

½ cup butter or margarine, softened

¾ cup sugar

1 egg

½ teaspoon almond extract

1 tablespoon maraschino cherry juice or syrup

1 to 2 drops pink gel food coloring

2 cups all-purpose flour

½ teaspoon baking soda

½ teaspoon salt

Crown-shaped cookie cutter

Pink sugar crystals

Silver decorating balls

Makes 12 (4-inch) cookies

Let's get baking!

Preheat oven to 375 degrees.

Cream butter or margarine in a large mixing bowl. Add sugar and beat until light and fluffy. Add egg, almond extract, maraschino cherry juice or syrup, and pink gel food coloring.

Combine flour, soda, and salt in a separate bowl. Add to creamed mixture and blend well.

Flatten out dough until it is about ¼ inch thick, cover with plastic wrap, and put in freezer for 15 minutes to chill.

Divide dough in half. Roll to ⅛ inch thick on lightly floured work area. Cut out with a crown-shaped cookie cutter and sprinkle liberally with pink sugar crystals. Press little silver decorating balls into the dough.

Place cookies 1 inch apart on cookie sheets sprayed with nonstick cooking spray. Bake for 8 to 10 minutes or until lightly browned.

Cute and sweet tiara treat!

Pretty Princess Puffs

Ingredients List

3 eggs whites

¾ cup sugar

¼ teaspoon cream of tartar

½ teaspoon vanilla or almond extract

2 to 3 drops assorted pastel gel food coloring

Confetti sprinkles, silver decorating balls, or pink sugar crystals

Makes 18 to 24 cookies

Let's get baking!

Preheat oven to 250 degrees. Line two cookie sheets with foil.

In a large bowl, whip egg whites with electric mixer until soft peaks form. With mixer on, slowly add sugar, a tablespoon at a time. Add cream of tartar, vanilla or almond extract, and gel food coloring. Continue beating until stiff peaks form.

Spoon mounds (about 2 tablespoons each) onto foil-lined cookie sheets; space them about ½ inch apart. Sprinkle with decoration of choice.

Place both cookie sheets on the middle rack of the preheated oven and bake for 1 hour. Then turn off oven and leave oven door closed for 10 minutes.

Remove puffs from baking sheets and store in an airtight container.

Melt-in-your-mouth perfection!

Raspberry Tea Sandwiches

Ingredients List

8 slices white bread

½ cup soft-spread cream cheese

1 tablespoon raspberry preserves

1 pint fresh raspberries

Colored sugar crystals or silver decorating balls

Makes 8 small sandwiches

Let's get spreading!

Cut bread into desired shapes with a cookie cutter.

In a small mixing bowl, combine cream cheese and raspberry preserves.

Spread a thin layer of the mixture on each bread cut-out, and then place raspberries on top of each sandwich.

Garnish each sandwich with a sprinkling of sugar crystals or silver decorating balls.

It's a tea party!

Classic Cucumber Sandwiches

Ingredients List

- 1 English (or seedless) cucumber

- 8 slices whole wheat or rye bread

- 2 tablespoons softened butter or mayonnaise

- Seasoned salt and pepper to taste

- Cherry tomatoes cut into pieces for garnish (optional)

- Edible flower petals* (optional) or mint sprigs

Makes 8 small sandwiches

*Ask an adult to help you get these. See note on page 64.

Let's get slicing!

Thinly slice 8 slices of cucumber and blot dr with a paper towel. Save the rest for another use

Cut crust off bread, and then cut out bread into assorted shapes with 2-inch cookie cutters.

Spread each little cut-out with butter or mayon naise. Lay cucumber slices on top.

Season with seasoning salt and pepper, and gar nish with a cherry tomato slice, edible flowe petals, or mint sprigs if desired.

Cute-as-a-cucumber!

Cheesy Biscuits

Ingredients List

½ cup butter, softened

2 cups grated cheddar cheese

1 tablespoon Worcestershire sauce

1 cup all-purpose flour

¼ teaspoon salt

Pinch cayenne pepper

Makes 10 to 12 biscuits

Let's get baking!

Preheat oven to 375 degrees.

In a large mixing bowl, combine butter, cheese, and Worcestershire sauce. Beat with an electric mixer on medium speed until all ingredients are well blended. Stir in flour, salt, and cayenne pepper.

Roll out or press out dough on a lightly floured work surface. Cut into assorted small shapes and place on a foil-lined baking sheet that has been very lightly sprayed with nonstick cooking spray.

Bake 10 to 12 minutes or until very lightly browned.

Little cheesy bites!

Candy-Coated Dragonflies

Ingredients List

8 to 10 squares vanilla candy coating or almond bark

Powdered food coloring* (optional)

8 (8-inch) pretzel rods

16 large pretzel twists

Assorted decorating sugars or sprinkles

Makes 8 dragonflies

*See note on page 64.

Don't let them fly away before you have a chance to take a bite!

Let's get melting!

Melt candy coating according to package directions. Remove from heat and pour into two or three small bowls. You may add 2 to 4 drops of food coloring to each bowl. Stir to blend color.

Place pretzel rods on a foil-lined cookie sheet sprayed with nonstick cooking spray (about 3 inches apart from each other). These are the dragonflies' long bodies.

Carefully spoon the warm melted candy coating over each pretzel rod to cover completely.

Dip each pretzel twist in the candy coating and place one on each side of the upper half of the pretzel rods. The pretzel twists should rest on top of the pretzel rods and just barely touch one another. These form the dragonflies' wings.

Sprinkle each dragonfly pretzel with decorating sugars or sprinkles.

Place cookie sheet in freezer for 5 to 10 minutes to allow candy coating to harden.

Remove from freezer and carefully take each dragonfly off cookie sheet to serve.

Little Ladybugs

Ingredients List

- 12 seedless red grapes
- 12 toothpicks
- 12 whole strawberries with stems
- 1 package mini-morsel chocolate chips

Makes 12 ladybugs

Let's go buggy!

Place a grape on a toothpick, sliding it all th way to the end of the stick. This is the ladybug head.

Next, place a strawberry on the toothpick, ster end first, and slide it down to touch the grap This is the ladybug's body.

Lay the ladybug down and carefully push th pointed ends of several chocolate chips into th strawberry to make the ladybug's spots.

Little ladybugs to decorate your plate!

Fairy-Tale Fondue

Ingredients List

cup heavy cream

2 ounces white
  chocolate, chopped

teaspoon vanilla

Makes about
1½ cups

Let's get melting!

Heat the cream in a medium saucepan over medium-low heat until hot, about 2 to 3 minutes. When hot, add the chocolate and stir until it is just melted and smooth. Stir in vanilla. Transfer to a warm fondue pot.

Serve with your choice of fresh strawberries, banana slices, apple wedges, pound cake, ladyfingers, and biscotti for dipping.

Make your own fairy-tale finger food!

Magic Princess Wands

Ingredients List

- ounces vanilla candy coating or almond bark
- owdered food coloring* (optional)
- large pretzel rods
- ssorted colored sugars, sprinkles, and sugar candy decorations

Makes 8 wands

See note on page 64.

Let's get dipping!

Melt white candy coating according to package directions. Add powdered food coloring if desired. Stir to blend.

Dip or drizzle pretzel rods with candy coating. Place coated pretzel rods on a foil-lined sheet pan that has been sprayed lightly with nonstick cooking spray. Decorate with sugars, sprinkles, or candies while candy coating is still warm.

Place sheet pan in freezer for 10 minutes to harden candy coating.

Remove and eat immediately or store in an airtight container for several days.

They're magical!

Blueberry Biscuits

Ingredients List

1 can large-size refrigerator biscuits

1 cup canned blueberry pie filling

¼ teaspoon ground nutmeg

¼ teaspoon almond extract

1 teaspoon ground cinnamon mixed with ¼ cup sugar

Makes 8 servings

Let's get baking!

Preheat oven to 375 degrees.

Spray a 12-cup muffin pan with nonstick cooling spray. Divide each biscuit in half. Press a half biscuit in the bottom of 8 of the muffin cups, covering bottom completely. Leave 4 of the cups empty.

In a small bowl, combine blueberry pie filling, nutmeg, and almond extract.

Spoon 1 tablespoon of the blueberry pie filling mixture on top of each biscuit half.

Cover the top of the blueberry filling with the remaining biscuit halves.

Sprinkle each biscuit with a little of the cinnamon-sugar mixture.

Bake for about 15 minutes. Serve warm.

Perfect for breakfast or an afternoon treat!

Bitsy Banana Bread Bites

Ingredients List

- bananas
- egg
- ½ cups all-purpose flour
- teaspoon baking powder
- cup sugar
- cup brown sugar
- teaspoon salt
- cup oil
- teaspoon vanilla
- cup pecans, mini chocolate chips, or dried cranberries (optional)
- Powdered sugar for dusting
- Small, fresh edible flowers* (optional)

Makes 24 mini muffins

*Ask an adult to help you get these. See note on page 64.

Let's get baking!

Preheat oven to 325 degrees.

Mash bananas in a mixing bowl.

Add remaining ingredients (except optional ingredients), stirring until just blended. Fold in pecans, mini chocolate chips, or dried cranberries if using.

Line a mini muffin tin with 24 paper liners or spray with nonstick cooking spray. Divide batter evenly between mini muffin cups.

Bake for 20 minutes. Remove from oven and cool. Dust with powdered sugar and garnish with a small, fresh edible flower if desired.

Fun in every tiny bite!

Star-Shine Strawberry Muffins

Ingredients List

- 1 cup all-purpose flour
- ¾ cup cornmeal
- ½ cup light brown sugar
- 2½ teaspoons baking powder
- ¼ teaspoon salt
- ¼ teaspoon cinnamon
- 1 (8-ounce) container low-fat strawberry yogurt
- ¼ cup butter, melted
- 1 egg
- 1 teaspoon vanilla
- 2 cups chopped fresh strawberries
- 6 strawberries, sliced into thin strips

Makes 12 muffins

Let's get baking!

Preheat oven to 350 degrees. Line a muffin pa with paper muffin cup liners and place on cookie sheet.

In a large bowl, whisk together flour, cornmea brown sugar, baking powder, salt, and cinnamon

Add yogurt, melted butter, egg, and vanilla. Mi well with a wooden spoon, making sure to blen all of the dry ingredients into the wet ingredi ents. Fold in chopped strawberries and spoo batter equally among 12 muffin cups, filling eac cup about three-fourths full.

Place 5 strawberry strips on top of each muffin t form star shapes.

Place cookie sheet in oven and bake for abou 25 minutes or until light golden brown. Remov from oven and cool for 5 minutes before remov ing muffins from pan. Serve with honey butter.

Make these the star of your party!

Chocolate Chip– Peppermint Scones

Ingredients List

½ cups all-purpose flour

cup sugar

teaspoons baking
powder

teaspoon salt

cup milk chocolate chips

cup plus 2 tablespoons
whipping cream

cup crushed peppermint
candies

owdered sugar for
dusting (optional)

Makes 12 scones

Let's get baking!

Preheat oven to 375 degrees.

In a large mixing bowl, stir together flour, sugar, baking powder, and salt until well combined. Add chocolate chips and toss to coat with flour mixture.

Pour 1 cup whipping cream into the mixture, stirring just until ingredients are moistened. Turn mixture out onto lightly floured surface. Knead gently until soft dough forms (about 2 minutes). Pat dough out to about 1 inch thick. Cut out into assorted shapes.

Place scones 1 inch apart on two foil-lined baking sheets that have been sprayed with nonstick cooking spray.

Brush each scone with the remaining 2 tablespoons whipping cream and sprinkle with crushed peppermint candies.

Bake 15 to 20 minutes or until very lightly browned. Serve warm and dusted with powdered sugar if desired.

Yummy peppermint treats!

Enchanted Unicorn Horns

Ingredients List

8 to 10 squares vanilla candy coating or almond bark

10 to 12 waffle or wafer-type ice cream cones with pointed ends

Assorted decorating sprinkles, placed in small saucers

Ice cream, frozen yogurt, or fruit sorbet

Makes 10 to 12 unicorn horns

Let's get dipping!

Melt vanilla candy coating or almond bark according to package directions.

Place melted candy coating in a medium-size bowl. Dip about 1½ to 2 inches of each cone (the big, open end) into melted candy coating.

Now take each dipped "unicorn horn" and dip the candy-covered end into decorating sprinkles.

Place each finished unicorn horn carefully on a foil-lined cookie sheet sprayed with nonstick cooking spray. Place in freezer 5 to 10 minutes to harden coating.

Remove unicorn horns from freezer. Fill each one with ice cream, frozen yogurt, or sorbet. Top with candy or additional sprinkles if desired.

So good they're enchanting!

Pink Princess Pudding

Ingredients List

small package vanilla instant pudding mix

teaspoon vanilla

ink gel food coloring

ecorating sugars or sprinkles (optional)

aspberries, maraschino cherries, or sliced strawberries (optional)

akes 4 servings

Let's get mixing!

Make pudding in a mixing bowl according to package directions, adding in the vanilla. Stir in 1 to 2 drops pink gel food coloring.

Chill and serve with optional garnishes as desired.

Pink and dreamy, smooth and creamy!

Ice Cream Sandwiches

Ingredients List

¼ cup butter or margarine (do not use soft-spread margarine)

1 (10-ounce) bag marshmallows

1 teaspoon vanilla

6 cups crispy rice cereal

½ cup decorating sprinkles (optional)

Ice cream

Makes 12 ice cream sandwiches

Let's get scooping!

Spray a medium saucepan with nonstick cooking spray. Melt butter or margarine with marshmallows in pan, stirring often. Stir in vanilla. Add cereal and remove from heat.

Stir together until a large ball begins to form. Add decorating sprinkles, if desired.

Scoop mix into a 9- x 13-inch pan that has been sprayed with nonstick cooking spray. Flatten, then chill in the refrigerator for 10 minutes. Remove from refrigerator and cut into 2-inch squares.

Put a small scoop of ice cream on top of one square and top with another square. Trim off extra ice cream so it is square. Press together and eat right away, or place in freezer until ready to serve.

A cool and crunchy confection!

Flowerpot Ice Cream

Ingredients List

- (3-inch) clay flowerpots
- cookies or 4 small pieces of cake
- ce cream, sorbet, or frozen yogurt
- hocolate syrup
- ssorted decorating sprinkles
- drinking straws, cut in half
- fresh or silk flowers

Iakes 4 servings

Let's get scooping!

Wash and dry new clay pots.

Place cookies or pieces of cake in the bottom of each clay pot. Press down, making sure they cover the hole in the bottom of each pot.

Put a scoop of ice cream into each flowerpot and drizzle with chocolate syrup. Decorate with sprinkles.

Insert a straw into the scoop of ice cream. Place the flower stem inside the straw.

Place each Flowerpot Ice Cream on a small saucer and serve. Flowerpot Ice Cream may be covered and stored in the freezer before inserting flowers into straws.

It's flowery fun!

Fancy Fruit Tarts

Ingredients List

- 1 package refrigerator piecrust dough
- Purchased "hardening shell" chocolate ice cream topping or vanilla yogurt
- Fresh fruit, washed and sliced or cut into bite-size pieces

Makes 12 tarts

A sweet fruit treat!

Let's get baking!

Unfold one piecrust at a time and place on lightly floured work surface.

Turn piecrust over to make sure both sides a lightly covered with flour. Gently roll o piecrust with rolling pin.

Using a 3-inch flower-shaped or round cook cutter, carefully cut out pieces of piecrust. Pla each cut-out crust in a 12-cup muffin pan th has been sprayed with nonstick cooking spr Continue until both piecrusts are used.

Prick bottoms of each piecrust with a for Place prepared muffin pan in refrigerator f 30 minutes to chill.

Preheat oven to 350 degrees. Remove muff pan from refrigerator, and bake tart shells oven for about 20 minutes or until gold brown. Remove from oven and cool 5 minute

Remove shells from pan and place on a servi plate. Spread bottom of each tart shell wi either the chocolate topping or a thin layer vanilla yogurt. Arrange fruits of your choice top and chill in the refrigerator for 10 minut or until ready to serve.

Lemonade Floats

Ingredients List

cup fresh lemon juice
  (about 10 to 12 lemons,
  squeezed)

cup honey or to taste

teaspoon vanilla

cup warm water

cups chilled sparkling
  water or club soda

ssorted fruit sorbets
  (lemon, lime, orange,
  raspberry, strawberry,
  and/or blueberry)

Makes 4 servings

Let's get mixing!

Combine lemon juice, honey, vanilla, and water in mixing bowl. Use whisk to blend ingredients.

Pour lemon juice mixture into a large pitcher and add chilled sparkling water or club soda, whisking to combine. Set pitcher in freezer for 5 minutes to cool quickly. Don't forget and leave it there!

While lemonade is chilling, choose your flavor—or combination of flavors—of sorbet. Using a melon baller, scoop 4 to 6 mini sorbet balls per serving. Place them inside each glass and pour sparkling lemonade on top.

Garnish with fresh fruit and a straw.

Float away to paradise!

Sparkling Princess Punch

Ingredients List

1 liter strawberry, raspberry, or lemon sparkling flavored water, chilled

1 small bottle maraschino cherries and juice

Juice of 1 lemon

Pink or purple colored sugar crystals (optional)

Makes 12 servings

Let's get chilling!

Combine chilled sparkling water, cherrie cherry juice, and lemon juice. Stir to blend.

Pour immediately into small punch cups or fanc juice glasses.

TIP: For a super-cool drinking glass, you ca turn any plain cup or glass into a "sugar sipper Before you fill the glass, just dampen the rim a the way around with the juice from a lim lemon, or orange. Pour about ¼ cup colore sugar onto a small plate. Dip the dampened ri of the drinking cup into the sugar. Voilà . . . sugar sipper!

A sparkling delight!

Rainbow Milks

Ingredients List

cup reduced-fat milk, soy milk, or chocolate milk

cup fresh or frozen fruit (peaches, bananas, strawberries, blueberries, or raspberries)

teaspoon vanilla or ¼ teaspoon almond extract

teaspoon sugar

ash of cinnamon or nutmeg

Makes 2 servings

Let's get blending!

Combine milk, fruit, and vanilla or almond extract in blender. Add sugar and cinnamon or nutmeg to taste.

Pour into a glass, add a straw, and drink it up!

TIP: Try chocolate milk with banana, vanilla, and cinnamon. Try regular milk with peaches, almond extract, and nutmeg. Try soy milk with strawberries and cinnamon.

They'll take you over the rainbow!

Mini-Marshmallow Smoothies

Ingredients List

1 ripe sliced banana

1 cup sliced strawberries

½ cup low-fat milk or vanilla soy milk

1 teaspoon vanilla

½ bag colored miniature marshmallows

Makes 4 servings

Let's get blending!

Place sliced banana and strawberries in an a tight container in freezer 15 minutes (or long before making smoothie.

Combine all ingredients, except marshmallow in blender and whirl until smooth and cream Stir in ½ cup of marshmallows.

Serve in small punch cups and garnish each wi a handful of marshmallows if desired.

TIP: For super-quick smoothies, keep slic frozen fruits in airtight containers in the freeze Just choose your fruits, add the other smooth ingredients, and you can make instant pure fru smoothies in a jiffy!

Mountains of marshmallows!